MY PET HUMAN

Yasmine Surovec

SQUARE
FISH

ROARING BROOK PRESS

New York

To Alex, Victor, Puppy, and our cats

SQUARE
FISH

An Imprint of Macmillan
175 Fifth Avenue
New York, NY 10010
mackids.com

Our books may be purchased in bulk for promotional, educational, or business use. Please contact
your local bookseller or the Macmillan Corporate and Premium Sales Department at
(800) 221-7945 ext. 5442 or by e-mail at MacmillanSpecialMarkets@macmillan.com.

Library of Congress Cataloging-in-Publication Data
Surovec, Yasmine, author, illustrator.
   My pet human / Yasmine Surovec.
      pages cm
   Summary: A cat that enjoys his carefree life gets some treats and backrubs from the humans
who have just moved into his favorite abandoned house, then sets out to train them properly, all
the while protesting to his friends that he has no interest in being tied down to a human pet.
      ISBN 978-1-250-08492-7 (paperback)   ISBN 978-1-62672-496-9 (ebook)
      [1. Cats—Fiction.]   I. Title

   PZ7.S965626My 2015
   [Fic]—dc23

2014042460

Originally published in the United States by Roaring Brook Press
First Square Fish Edition: 2016
Book designed by Roberta Pressel
Square Fish logo designed by Filomena Tuosto

10 9 8 7 6 5

LEXILE: 470L

CONTENTS

CHAPTER 1
Mr. Independent

I'm a lucky cat. I live a carefree life.

This is my territory. I know these streets like the back of my paw. Lots of cats are tied down by staying with their pet humans, but not me. I'm my own cat, and the only one I have to look out for is myself. I wouldn't have it any other way.

All I have to do is follow a few rules to stay on easy street.

DOWNTOWN

THE TWIRLING FORK

SUPERMARKET WITH FREE SAMPLES

AWESOME CHINESE FOOD

First, know the good places in town to eat. The supermarket has free samples, and the dumpster at the Chinese restaurant is full of leftovers too.

But the Twirling Fork is the best place to find grub: spaghetti and meatballs, pizza, roasted chicken . . . all the good stuff!

I just wait at the back of the restaurant until I see someone take a break. It's usually one of the cooks or waiters.

Once he sees me, I give him "the Look."

It took me a while to master "the Look," but it's essential to getting what I want from humans. And let's just say, I always get what I want. I mean, who can resist this face? I'm adorable!

"The Look" doesn't seem to work on all humans. See that truck right there patrolling the neighborhood? That's bad news right there. The man inside rides around town looking for cats and dogs. He traps them in little cages and takes them to the pound!

I've heard that in the pound, hundreds of cats and dogs in cages are crying and howling to get out.

I've never been there but I'd rather not find out the hard way if it's true. That's why the #1 rule of the street is STAY ALERT!

This leads to the next rule: always have a good hiding spot.

I like the tree across from the empty house on the corner. No one has lived there for ages. The tree is perfect for a cat like me.

My last rule for a happy, carefree life is to have a few trusty friends. This yellow house is my friend Ben's place. It's really big and fancy.

And this is Ben, aka Mr. Fluffypuffypaws. He's got a lot of pet humans.

He has to deal with them every day. Or until they go to bed. IF they go to bed.

In Ben's backyard is a sweet doghouse where Ben hangs out to get away from it all. It's also where I usually meet up with him and a couple of other friends.

Farrah lives with her pet human in that white glass box on top of the hill.

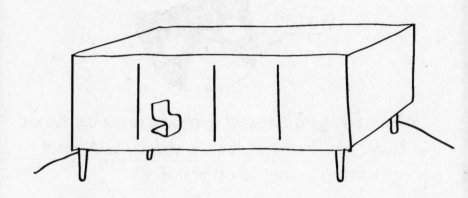

Her human spoils her and gives her whatever she wants.

MY HUMAN LOVES FANCY AND EXPENSIVE THINGS. AND SHE LOVES ME, SO SHE GETS ME THE BEST TREATS AND TOYS.

SHE WORKS HARD ALL DAY. SO WHEN SHE GETS HOME, I'LL SIT ON HER LAP AND PURR TO HELP HER RELAX.

And this is George. George lives with a little boy and his dad in a small apartment on the other side of town.

But unlike Ben's crazy kids, George's pet human is extremely quiet and shy. He's so shy that he locks himself in his bedroom most days to play video games.

Sometimes, my friends ask me why I don't get my own pet human. They just don't know how hard it would be to find one right for me!

My pet human would have to be perfect! He or she MUST:

1) Feed me LOTS of treats

2) Give me back rubs

SCRITCH SCRITCH

3) Have plenty of boxes for me to play with

4) Be lots of fun

5) NOT smoosh me on the face, squeeze me too tightly, or pull my whiskers and tail

6) Let me sleep on his or her lap

7) Feed me a LOT!

8) Be a good and faithful companion

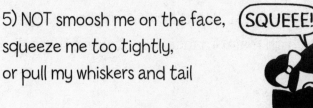

The perfect human just doesn't exist. They're crazy, aloof, moody, or high maintenance. I don't want to deal with that.

My friends just don't understand. I like living alone.

When they go back to their humans for the night, there's plenty I can do myself.

I can go to the Twirling Fork. I can find a tree to sleep in. I can—

Wait, where did he come from? Run!

Phew! I lost him. I have to be careful. No one is looking out for me except me.

I've had some close calls with the law, but I make sure I never get caught.

PHEW! WITH MY AMAZING AGILITY AND SPEED, I WAS ABLE TO OUTRUN HIM!

Sure, there are some benefits to having a pet human,
like animal control would leave me alone. But no human
can pin me down. I love my freedom way too much. I'm
better off on my own.

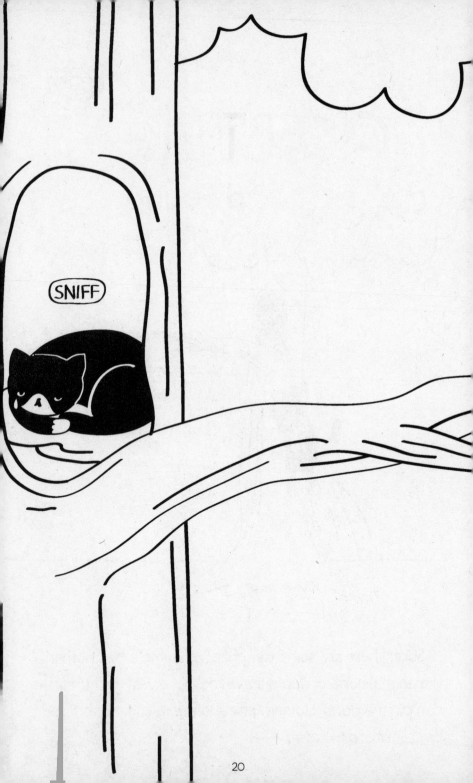

CHAPTER 2
Lost and Found

People are moving into the abandoned house. Maybe I should investigate.

I smell something awesome. My nose is telling me that the scent is coming from that house. I missed dinner last night and I'm starving!

Hm, I see a little human girl . . . with a bowl of macaroni and cheese topped with TUNA! I must get my paws on that!

This is a challenge. Little humans tend to be a bit nutty.

But it's nothing I can't handle. Watch a master at work.

I pop in the window and settle by her feet.

Major charm is the trick to getting what I want.

Remember "the Look" I talked about earlier? It's time to unleash it.

The weepy, doe-eyed look gets me what I want almost every time.

It's kind of weird being ogled at while I'm eating, but I'm so hungry, I'll ignore her.

IF YOU'RE STILL A BIT HUNGRY, THERE'S ONE LAST CAN OF TUNA IN THE CUPBOARD.

OH, AND HERE, TRY SOME OLIVES. WE HAVE LOTS!

AFTERWARD, I HAVE A BOX FOR YOU TO PLAY WITH!

I'VE ALWAYS WANTED A KITTY!

I WONDER WHAT AN OLIVE IS.

HM! TASTY!

An older human comes into the room. Unlike the little human, she's a little bit more, um, unfriendly. But that's okay. I'll just gobble up this bowl of food and then I'm outta here.

ACK! WHY IS THAT STRAY CAT IN THE HOUSE?

AW, MOM! DON'T SCARE HIM AWAY!

ISN'T HE CUTE?

I think it's time to go! I pretty much just stuck around for the grub.

HEY! WHERE ARE YOU GOING?

I'VE GOT MORE TUNA!

AND OLIVES!

OH, MOM, CAN WE KEEP HIM?

Tuna? Olives? If she insists!

SOMEONE ELSE MIGHT BE LOOKING FOR HIM. SO MAKE SURE TO HANG SOME "CAT FOUND" POSTERS AROUND THE BLOCK JUST TO MAKE SURE.

OKAY, LET ME GET MY CAMERA.

I don't think they understand that I'm not hanging around much longer. I just stopped by for tuna . . .

. . . and this thing, whatever it is.

CAT FOUND

IS THIS YOUR KITTY?

FOUND ON CENTRAL
AND 3RD.

HE'S A TUXEDO CAT
AND HE LOVES TO EAT!

IF HE IS YOURS,
CALL 555-8642.

OKAY, NOW YOU BE A GOOD BOY WHILE I HEAD OUT AND HANG THESE POSTERS.

MOM WILL BE WATCHING YOU WHILE I'M GONE.

She definitely doesn't understand that I'm not staying or that no one's looking for me. In the meantime, I'll stick around and play with these boxes.

OKAY, MISTER, TIME FOR A BATH.

NOPE! This is not my idea of a good time!

Ick. I hate getting wet!
Yeesh! Baths are the worst!

Humans and their baths . . . I don't get it. This is not how I clean myself!

THERE, ALL CLEAN.

THIS MUST BE WHAT A BURRITO FEELS LIKE.

But I like these cozy boxes. I'll probably have time for a little cat nap before I go.

CHAPTER 3
How to Train a Human

This human thinks that she can bribe me into staying forever with food.

And back rubs! Hmm . . . some humans aren't as annoying as I'd thought.

Oh look, my friends are here!

Hi, Ben! Hi, Farrah! Hi, George!

Staying at the humans' house has been a blast, and it's not as bad as I'd imagined it would be. But I was glad to see my friends.

Ben and Farrah and George had lots of questions for me. They were kinda surprised that I was hanging out with some humans.

YEAH, BUT THESE HUMANS AREN'T CRAZY. THE LITTLE HUMAN I MET DOESN'T SMOTHER ME TO PIECES.

But I told them about the boxes...

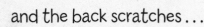

and the back scratches...

and most importantly, the bowls of olives and tuna and mac 'n' cheese!

They still didn't get it.

WHATEVER. KNOWING HOW YOU ARE, YOU'RE GONNA LEAVE ONCE THE TUNA RUNS OUT.

AW, DON'T BE TOO HARD ON THE GUY.

Hm. Now I don't know what to do. Part of me is thinking that I shouldn't stay too long and warm up to these humans. I mean, I'm my own cat, and I don't need to be responsible for a pet human! But another part of me is saying this is a pretty sweet set-up.

Going about town looking for food can be tiring. Sure, humans are unpredictable, but what if . . . I can train them? Now training a human to feed me all the treats that I want, I can see that happening.

I don't take off. I go inside instead.

I can definitely train this little human to be my pet.
She already adores me.

How difficult can it be to give me treats on demand?

First, I try purring.

When that doesn't work, I try meowing. A lot.

Sometimes humans are kinda slow to get things.

When all else fails, I give her "the Look."

See? It works! And to reward her, I give her a head boop to show my appreciation.

And that is how to train a human. Persistence. Patience. And rewards for good behavior.

It's just that simple.

Now, if I'm going to stay here, I also need to train the mother human. While the little human is easy to train, the mom is a bit more . . . challenging. Older humans tend to be set in their ways.

She's no fun at all.

She tends to bark orders.

And she gets annoyed easily.

ACK! THAT'S CLEAN LAUNDRY!

But I can change all that! With a little time and patience, I can get any human to warm up. How? It's the simple gestures that make a big difference.

WHAT TH–?

For example, I know the mother human likes it when I swish my tail against her face, especially when she's trying to read or getting ready for bed.

All humans like presents. I give her a present from my daily adventures as an expert domestic hunter. Humans, after all, make horrible hunters.

My most favorite animals to hunt are vicious snakes caught in the wild, like underneath the flower pot in the backyard.

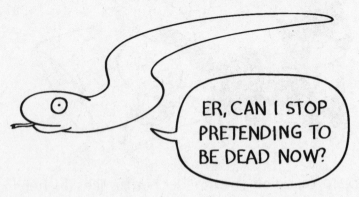

I can tell she's excited by my present!

Or maybe not. Some humans are hard to please.

Lastly, remember how a cat's belly is irresistible to humans?

I've been told that my belly is soft as a fluffy cloud. No one can resist my magical belly. Not even grumpy humans.

See? It's easy to get humans to warm up. Like I said, it just takes a little time, a little effort, and a lot of smarts (which is something I have tons of).

In no time, I'll have these pet humans wrapped around my furry little paws. I've been staying here for several days, and I gotta admit, life has been good. I've got toys and treats and tuna and olives, and I don't even have to go scrounging around town to find them!

But of course my friends come over and check up on me. And they have a thing or two to say. "It's not always about you," Ben tells me.

But I don't have a pet human. I'm just hanging out here for a while until I figure out what I want to do. In the meantime, I have a little human I've trained to give me what I want.

YOU HAVE A CARD FROM ONE OF YOUR FRIENDS BACK HOME.

I guess I'll get more tuna and olives and back scratches if the humans under my training are A-OK. It's just that as I've mentioned before, humans tend to be a bit moody.

SIGH.

CHAPTER 4
Operation Find-a-Friend

Lately, all the little human does is sulk.

I have to fix her. Maybe my irresistible charm will do the trick!

I try purring loudly
and rolling on the floor
to show how cute I
am. After all, the little
human likes cute things.

I lend her my
favorite toys.

I've been told that I
have a beautiful voice,
so I sing her a song.

I show her this funny-looking spider I found hanging on the window sill.

I mean, he's funny-looking!

I even bring her THIS AWESOME BOX! Who doesn't love a good ol' box?

I guess she doesn't.

When I'm feeling down, I go see Ben, Farrah, and George. They're good friends. They are always there for me.

Little human should have friends just like I do. Then she wouldn't be so sad.

They could play in boxes.

Look for bugs in the grass.

And eat tuna fish sandwiches with olives!

That's my new plan. It isn't going to be easy, but I'm going to help her make a new friend!

I would ask Ben. He's got a whole bunch of little humans—maybe they could be her friends. But they're on vacation.

WHEEEE!

I'll ask Farrah. She's not usually around little humans, but she might have a helpful suggestion.

TRY ASKING GEORGE. HE'S GOT A LITTLE HUMAN SHE COULD BE FRIENDS WITH, BUT IT MAY TAKE A BIT MORE WORK SINCE HIS HUMAN USUALLY KEEPS TO HIMSELF.

George likes my idea to get his human and my human to hang out. So we come up with an elaborate plan, which involves a lot of wit and cunning, something George and myself both have tons of.

I HOPE THIS INVOLVES CHEESE AND CRACKERS. HUMANS LOVE CHEESE AND CRACKERS.

UH, NO. IT'S A BIT MORE COMPLICATED THAN THAT.

Now let Operation Find-a-Friend begin!
I need something of value, something to use as bait.

I know exactly what to use.

This should lure her out of the house.

Now that I've got her outside, I need to make sure she's headed toward George's apartment. Hopefully George has stuck to the plan.

George's job was to lure his little human outside, which I'm sure wasn't easy. His human hardly ever leaves the house.

I throw my human's hat into the bush too. That's the last part of the plan.

See, the way Operation Find-a-Friend works is, you take two shy kids out of their comfort zones, and, somehow, get them to meet up. It's a bit tricky, really.

But we can always hope that it works!

And it did! Look at their happy faces.

And now a beautiful friendship begins, I hope.

George and I couldn't believe it. His human is . . . talking. They're having an actual conversation!

There's nothing more satisfying than executing a plan perfectly! We actually got our humans to become friends.

They're going inside George's building. I think they are going to read comic books.

SLAM!

GOSH, I DON'T THINK I'VE SEEN LIAM THIS EXCITED BEFORE!

Things worked out really well. I knew it would! I mean, I never doubted for a second.

But wait a minute. My human is gone.

Really, what do I care? My job here is done. My friends are happy. The little humans are happy.

Time for me to move along, I suppose.

CHAPTER 5

My Pet Human

My human hasn't even come out to look for me. I guess she found a new friend. She doesn't need me anymore.

I think of the tuna. I think of the olives. I think of the boxes. I think of my little human. It was just too good to be true.

I guess I'm off . . . I shouldn't be too sad. I'm a cat!

Good thing I don't have a pet human to worry about! If no one has time for me, then I don't have time for them. So off I go!

Look out world, here I come!

I remember our good times together. I remember our head boop.

Oh well. Since I'm back on my own, I can't forget the first rule of the street: stay alert!

Oh no! Animal Control!
I zig. I zag.
But I can't avoid the net.

HISss!

THIS
CAN'T
BE
HAPPENING!!!

THIS IS HORRIBLE! I've had nightmares about this, and it never ends well.

Wh-what's going to happen to me?!
I can almost hear the cries from the pound already.

This is not how I wanted things to end! I want to go home! I want my friends! I wanna get outta here!

I'M GONNA DIE ALONE!!!

Wait . . . I hear someone outside the truck.

I hear yelling. I hear the little human's voice.

Is she here to get me out? Please save me! I can't spend the rest of my life in cat jail. PLEASE!

No, don't listen to anything Animal Control has to say!

I hear another voice. It sounds familiar. Is it ... little human's MOTHER?

THAT'S RIGHT! HE'S OUR CAT. I'VE BEEN LOOKING EVERYWHERE FOR HIM.

OH.

I thought she HATED me. Wow, she sure did a good job playing hard to get. Now please! Get me outta this place!

And the moment I heard the click, I just knew.

THERE YOU ARE!

I had my pet human.

And she is perfect in every way.

It's not just my little human and my big human there either. It's all my friends! Ben, Farrah, George, and George's pet human, Liam. They all came to save me!

HEY! YOU SHOULD COME OVER TO OUR HOUSE TOMORROW.

WE HAVE AN INFLATABLE POOL IN OUR BACKYARD!

OKAY, I'LL BRING MY GOGGLES.

I GUESS IT'S TIME TO TAKE DOWN THOSE "MISSING CAT" SIGNS.

My pet human hugs me tight and carries me home.

She wants to give me a name. Little human isn't very good with names. While she thinks about it, I've already decided what to call her. She looks like a Freckles to me. Because, you know, she has freckles. So I'll be calling her that.

She thinks about names for a long time. While she's
rubbing my belly. While she's washing dishes . . .

While she's feeding me tuna and olives . . .

And then finally she gets it right.

The End

GO FISH

YASMINE SUROVEC

Photo by Victor Surovec

What did you want to be when you grew up?
I wanted to be an animator, a toy designer, a cartoonist, and an illustrator. I went to art school, so after I graduated, I fulfilled (most of) my dreams and became a toy designer, a cartoonist, and an illustrator!

When did you realize you wanted to be a writer?
I'd like to think that I make stories using images, because I make comics primarily. And I always loved comics as a child and always wanted to make my own since then. When I was in grade school, we'd have writers' workshops, and it was my absolute favorite, because we got to write, draw, and tell stories.

What's your most embarrassing childhood memory?
I sat on a chair with a big blob of ice cream spilled on the seat! And a lot of my classmates saw it!

What's your favorite childhood memory?
I have so many! As a child, I lived in the Philippines. And my first trip to the United States to visit family and friends was one of my favorites.

As a young person, who did you look up to most?

My parents. I admire them for working very hard so that my brother, sister, and I could have a good education, good food, nice clothes, and a nice, safe place to live. They are also very talented. My dad is an architect and my mom is an animator. Seeing them work, I've always wanted to be in a creative field like them.

What was your favorite thing about school?

I was quite shy when I was a kid, so I loved reading the books we had at school. One of my favorite books was *A Wrinkle in Time* by Madeleine L'Engle. Discovering new books is awesome! And when you're in school, you have access to lots of new books.

What were your hobbies as a kid? What are your hobbies now?

As a kid, I made my own comics. I also loved to paint and draw. Since I had lots of family members who worked in the creative industry, I always had lots of art supplies.

My hobbies right now are pretty much the same. My comic, *Cat Versus Human*, started out as a hobby, which became a full-time job. I love making comics, and I hope to do so for a long time.

Did you play sports as a kid?

Not much. I wasn't the sportiest kid.

What was your first job, and what was your "worst" job?

My first job after college was as an illustrator for a toy company. It was awesome!

I wouldn't say that I've had worse jobs. I treat them all as a learning experience, so hopefully I can keep getting better with my skills.

What book is on your nightstand now?
I have a little son now, and we read to him quite a bit. And a book that's on top of my shelf is *The Shy Little Kitten*, illustrated by Gustaf Tenggren with the story by Cathleen Schurr. It's a Little Golden Books book, and it's a super-cute read.

How did you celebrate publishing your first book?
I don't quite remember. We lived in the Bay Area at the time, so we probably just had dinner at a nice restaurant.

Where do you write your books?
I have a home office where I write and illustrate my books. But when ideas pop up, regardless of where I am, I jot them down so I don't forget about them.

What sparked your imagination for *My Pet Human*?
I have lots of cats! And if you've ever had a cat in your life, sometimes it feels like the cats "own" you or consider you their pet, rather than the other way around.

What challenges do you face in the writing process, and how do you overcome them?
At this time, maybe scheduling. I work on multiple projects at once, so I try to make sure to prioritize, based on when things are due.

What is your favorite word?
My favorite word is "gigil" (pronounced *ghee-gil*). It is a word in Tagalog that I don't think has a translation in English. It means an overwhelming feeling that may cause one to have

an irresistible urge to pinch, hug, or squeeze something that is too cute. Kind of like that feeling you have when you see a cute kitten!

My other favorite word, which is in English, is "purr."

If you could live in any fictional world, what would it be?

Oh, any world created by Hayao Miyazaki. I love all his movies, like *Spirited Away*, *Princess Mononoke*, and *Howl's Moving Castle*. He makes such magical worlds, and they're places I would absolutely love to visit.

In literature, I'd probably want to retrace Alice's steps in Wonderland. That would be an interesting trip!

Who is your favorite fictional character?

There's just so many. I love books with strong female leads. But I also love a good period love story. So I'd say Elizabeth Bennet from *Pride and Prejudice*.

In film, it would be Princess Nausicaä from *Nausicaä of the Valley of the Wind*.

What was your favorite book when you were a kid? Do you have a favorite book now?

I loved *A Wrinkle in Time* when I was an older kid. But when I was a younger kid, I liked *Tikki Tikki Tembo*, *Caps for Sale*, and the Dr. Seuss books. I also loved book collections of Asian folklore.

If you could travel in time, where would you go and what would you do?

I'd like to go back to Spanish pre-colonial times. I absolutely love history, and seeing cultures and events as they unfold at that time would be amazing.

SQUARE FISH

What's the best advice you have ever received about writing?
"Just write." I interpreted that as writing whatever is in your heart, putting it on paper or typing on the computer, regardless of grammatical errors and such. Because there's always room for revision later on.

What advice do you wish someone had given you when you were younger?
That I shouldn't stress out too much about trying to fit in. Being yourself makes you unique!

Do you ever get writer's block? What do you do to get back on track?
Yes! To overcome this, I either work on a project unrelated to writing, or maybe take a brief rest. Sometimes my brain just gets overwhelmed and I need to unwind.

What do you want readers to remember about your books?
I hope my readers find some humor in my books. And hopefully, they see themselves in them, too.

What would you do if you ever stopped writing?
I can't see that happening. But if it did, I would go back to being a toy or accessories designer.

If you were a superhero, what would your superpower be?
I'd love to be able to fly!

Do you have any strange or funny habits? Did you when you were a kid?
I bit my nails as a kid. But that's not too strange, though.

What do you consider to be your greatest accomplishment?
Just being happy, and making the most out of life.

What would your readers be most surprised to learn about you?
I've made my own cowboy boots from scratch!

When Freckles signs up for a pet talent show, Oliver supposes he could help out. But when Freckles takes in a foster kitten, Oliver's suddenly not so eager to give up center stage!

MY PET HUMAN
Takes Center Stage

Written and Illustrated by
Yasmine Surovec

Read on for an excerpt!

An Annoying Guest

Saturday morning, Freckles's mom goes to the shelter. Ugh. I'm not looking forward to meeting the kitten.

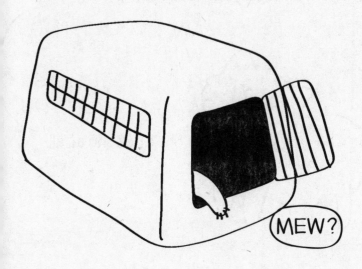

I'll bet she's going to be a gross and ugly kitten and she's going to scare Freckles away.

See how annoying and hideous she is?

She's not shy at all.

She plays with
my favorite box.

She eats my kibble.

She just arrived, and she already acts as if she
owns the place.

She's got my humans wrapped around her little paw.

She is NOT the cutest little thing.
I'M the cutest little thing!

It seems like Freckles can't get enough of her though.

The little kitten tries to snuggle up with me too. Yuck. I'd rather snuggle with a pineapple.

I'm outta here. I'm heading out to Ben's.